Makeover Magic

✱ . . ✱ . . ✱ . ✱ . . ✱ . . ✱

Book 3

Makeover Magic

JILL SANTOPOLO

Aladdin

NEW YORK LONDON TORONTO SYDNEY NEW DELHI

ALADDIN
An imprint of Simon & Schuster Children's Publishing Division
1230 Avenue of the Americas, New York, NY 10020
First Aladdin paperback edition June 2014
Text copyright © 2014 by Simon & Schuster, Inc.
Cover illustrations and interior spot illustrations copyright © 2014 by Cathi Mingus
All rights reserved, including the right of reproduction in whole or in part in any form.
ALADDIN is a trademark of Simon & Schuster, Inc., and related logo is
a registered trademark of Simon & Schuster, Inc.
Also available in an Aladdin hardcover edition.
For information about special discounts for bulk purchases, please contact
Simon & Schuster Special Sales at 1-866-506-1949 or business@simonandschuster.com.
The Simon & Schuster Speakers Bureau can bring authors to your live event. For more
information or to book an event, contact the Simon & Schuster Speakers Bureau
at 1-866-248-3049 or visit our website at www.simonspeakers.com.
Series and cover designed by Jeanine Henderson
The text of this book was set in Adobe Caslon.
Manufactured in the United States of America 0615 OFF
10 9 8 7 6 5 4 3 2
Library of Congress Control Number 2014933118
ISBN 978-1-4424-7387-4 (hc)
ISBN 978-1-4424-7386-7 (pbk)
ISBN 978-1-4424-7388-1 (eBook)

For my community of friends and family.

I'd love to give each and every one of you an On the Ball trophy.

And extra-special thanks to Karen Nagel,

Marianna Baer, Betsy Bird, and Eliot Schrefer,

who help Aly and Brooke (and me!) to sparkle.

Contents

Chapter 1   I'm So Grapeful   1

Chapter 2   Kiss and Tell   14

Chapter 3   Candy Corn on the Cob   23

Chapter 4   Apple Crispy   33

Chapter 5   Pickle Me   40

Chapter 6   Midnight Blues   57

Chapter 7   Plum Delicious   65

Chapter 8   Very Ice Try   73

Chapter 9   Heavy Metal   84

Chapter 10   News Prince   95

Chapter 11   Good Knight   104

How to Give Yourself (or a Friend!)
   a Caramel-Dipped Pedicure   113

one

I'm So Grapeful

Aly Tanner glanced at her purple polka-dot watch. *Uh-oh.* She and her sister, Brooke, had only four minutes to unpack the new polish colors before their first appointments showed up at Sparkle Spa.

"Brooke," Aly said, looking to where her sister was carefully reorganizing the bottles at the polish display, "we've got to go a little faster. Jenica and Bethany are going to be here for their pedicures soon. And then the rest of the soccer team will be coming in all afternoon."

Sparkly, the girls' tiny dog, who lived in Sparkle Spa during the day and at home with them at night, barked in agreement.

"I know, I know," Brooke said. "But I just can't decide if I'm So Grapeful should go before Plum Delicious or after We the Purple. It's hard to tell how the color's going to come out on people's nails. And I want the display to be absolutely right so that no one thinks they're getting one color and ends up getting another."

Aly smiled. Brooke's attention to detail was partially what made Sparkle Spa look so beautiful— she'd been in charge of picking the paintings on the walls, the colorful pillows in the nail-drying and bracelet-making area, and the huge rainbow display of polish. Aly quickly opened up a bottle of I'm So Grapeful and brushed it onto her thumbnail. Then she blew on it and added a second coat.

"Does this help?" she asked. "Can you tell better now?"

Brooke's eyes lit up. "Yes. Now I know exactly where it should go." She slid the bottle in right next to Purple People Eater and went on to the next color.

"You know," Aly said, handing Brooke Cider Donuts, which was a very light orange, and Apple Crispy, which was a bright red, "I think later we should pull out all the colors that have to do with fall stuff. You know, for the Sixth-Grade Fall Ball."

"Okay," said Brooke. "And maybe we can come up with some special Fall Ball combinations."

"Maybe tomorrow?" Aly asked. "When Sparkle Spa is closed?"

Brooke nodded as she put a bright yellowish-gold polish called Candy Corn on the Cob next to Lemon Aid. Sparkle Spa, which was really just the back room of True Colors, Aly and Brooke's mom's nail salon, had a lot of rules. One of them was that the girls could be open only two days after school and one day during the weekend. That was so they could still do homework and hang out with their friends.

"I can't wait until I'm in sixth grade and can go to the Fall Ball," Brooke said, reaching for a silvery Very Ice Try. "Only three more years."

Aly closed the box and put it in the corner with the rest of the extra polish bottles. "And only two more years until you get to decorate. I can't believe I get to be a decorator this year."

The Sixth-Grade Fall Ball was one of the biggest events of the school year at Auden Elementary. The fifth graders always decorated the gym for the dance. It was tradition. It was also tradition that two sixth graders, one girl and one boy, got trophies for being "On the Ball." They were chosen by teachers and always had to be kids who were good students and good friends and gave back to the school community. Aly wondered who was going to get the trophies this year.

"Are you guys open yet?" a voice called from the Sparkle Spa doorway. It was Jenica Posner:

- sixth-grade captain of the girls' soccer team
- the most popular girl at Auden Elementary
- and Sparkle Spa's very first customer, back when Aly and Brooke started the salon a little more than a month ago.

Jenica was also the person Aly would vote for to win one of the On the Ball trophies if winners were chosen by students instead of teachers.

Jenica was more than just a great soccer player. She had also created an after-school program called

Superstar Sports. Two days a week, she and a group of volunteers helped the younger kids at school learn how to play soccer and kickball and practice things like teamwork and good sportsmanship.

"We're open!" Brooke said. "And we have lots of new colors. The polish company is really pushing a fall theme this year."

"We thought some of these would be perfect for the ball," Aly added, securing her chin-length hair in a half-up so it wouldn't fall in her face while she was polishing.

"Sounds cool—can I see?" Jenica asked.

"But you're still going to get the rainbow sparkle pedicure today, right?" Brooke said, handing over a bottle of Cider Donuts.

"Absolutely," Jenica answered, slipping off her sneakers and socks. "Otherwise, we might kill our winning streak." Ever since Jenica and the other soccer players had started getting rainbow sparkle pedicures, they'd won every single soccer game they'd played. The girls said it was because their feet had sparkle power, but Aly was pretty sure it was just because they were really good soccer players.

Still, she liked having so many regular customers at Sparkle Spa and especially liked hanging out with Jenica Posner. Sometimes she still couldn't believe that the two of them were friends.

"But," Jenica continued, jumping up into a pedi-cure chair, "I'm thinking I might get something different for the Fall Ball. Because I just bought my shoes—silver sandals with little heels. It's the first time I'm allowed to wear heels."

"Really?" Bethany asked, walking into Sparkle Spa. "My glamma got me my first pair of high heels when I was six. But they were for dress-up only."

"Your glamma?" Brooke asked.

"Yeah, 'glamorous' plus 'grandma' equals 'glamma,'" Bethany said. She sat down in the chair next to Jenica and unbuckled her sandals, and Aly and Brooke started the sparkle pedicures. "My glamma is super-glamorous. She was even in a television commercial once."

Aly thought about her own grandma, who wore jeans and sweatshirts and was not very glamorous at all. She'd never been on TV, either. Aly decided she liked it that way.

"Which boy do you think is going to get the On the Ball trophy?" Bethany asked.

"Everyone thinks it's going to be Lucas," Jenica answered. Aly had never spoken to Lucas Grant, but she knew who he was. He played basketball and the trumpet, and all the girls called him "Cute Lucas" because, well, he was really handsome. He'd also started a program called Reading Buddies, where sixth graders went into the kindergarten classes to read to the kids. It was a pretty cool program, and Aly hoped it would still be going next year so she could volunteer for it.

"I think it's going to be Oliver," Bethany replied, looking at her toes.

"That's just because you like him," Jenica said, rolling her eyes.

"Well, he's very likeable!" Bethany answered. Aly was pretty sure she was blushing. "But still, I think he has a good chance. He was the one who got the cafeteria to donate its extra food to homeless shelters, after all. That does more for the community than reading to little kids."

Just as Aly and Brooke were applying the top coat of clear polish to the rainbow sparkle pedicures, Mia, their next appointment, ran into the spa. Anjuli, the team's goalie, was right behind her.

"Guys," Mia said dramatically, standing in the

middle of the doorframe, "I have crazy news."

"What?" Brooke asked, whipping around to face Mia.

Aly twisted her head to look at Mia too.

From his fenced-in corner, Sparkly even turned to see what was happening.

"Princess Polish just opened!" Mia said. "Can you believe it?"

Sparkly whimpered and turned back around.

Aly and Brooke exchanged a Secret Sister Eye Message that meant: *Oh no!*

Princess Polish was a new nail salon across the street that'd had a COMING SOON sign in the window for the last month or so. It had worried Aly and Brooke's mom for a while, but then it seemed like it might never open. Now it had. This was not good news for Sparkle Spa. Or for Mom's salon, True Colors.

"Does it look any good?" Bethany asked. "My cousin told me there's a Princess Polish in her town and it's really awesome."

"Bethany!" Jenica elbowed her. "It won't be any better than Sparkle Spa."

"Sheesh," Bethany said, rubbing her arm. "I was just asking."

Aly had to bite her cheek not to smile. She loved how loyal a customer Jenica was.

"But I didn't even tell you the craziest part yet!" Mia still hadn't moved from the doorframe, and Anjuli was still behind her. "They're offering a *free* Princess Pedicure to anyone under thirteen who goes into the salon! And a manicure, too, if you're going to Auden's Fall Ball. How did they even know about our school's dance?"

Aly gulped. This was even worse news. It wasn't like they charged a lot at Sparkle Spa; in fact, that was one of Mom's rules—there was no set price, just a donation jar for customers to pay whatever they could afford. Then, each time the jar reached $100, Aly and Brooke gave the money to a worthy cause. So far, they'd donated money to Paws for Love, an animal shelter on Taft Street. The jar was getting kind of full again. They'd have to pick another charity soon.

"Wow," Bethany said. "That's a really nice offer."

"Right?" Mia said.

Jenica glared at them. Then she cleared her throat. "Aly, Brooke, I'd like to book my appointment for a manicure and pedicure for the Fall Ball. Here at Sparkle Spa. Can I book it now?"

Aly smiled at Jenica. She let out a breath she didn't know she was holding. "You definitely can," she said, pulling out the new appointment book Mom had gotten them just for Sparkle Spa. Mom reviewed it every week to make sure there weren't too many appointments for the girls to handle. "When would you like to come?"

"Next Saturday morning at eleven," Jenica answered, after thinking for a bit. "We have an early soccer game, but I'll be free after that."

"You got it," Aly said, writing her into the book.

"Me too," Anjuli said from where she stood behind Mia. "I'll come at eleven thirty."

"And me," Mia said after Aly had finished writing. "I'll come at the same time as Anjuli."

Bethany didn't say anything, though, no matter how hard Jenica glared at her. And if Bethany, one of their regulars, wanted to check out Princess Polish, Aly knew they had a problem brewing. A big one.

two

Kiss and Tell

The problem followed the Tanners home. That night, Mom was not in the very best mood. The minute she and the girls and Sparkly arrived home, she grabbed the cordless phone, went into her bedroom, and called Aly and Brooke's dad. He was away on a business trip and wouldn't be back until the weekend.

Brooke and Aly stayed in the living room, playing fetch with Sparkly. They'd trained him so that when Brooke threw a tiny ball, Sparkly would get it and bring it to Aly. And then when Aly threw it, he'd bring the ball to Brooke. It had taken ages for Sparkly to learn that.

"You think Mom is talking to Dad about Princess Polish?" Brooke asked as she threw the ball.

"Probably," Aly said, taking it from Sparkly's mouth and throwing it again.

"Do you think—" Brooke held on to the ball until Sparkly barked, and then she threw it. "Do you think Princess Polish could ever be more popular than True Colors? And if that happened, would True Colors close? And then Sparkle Spa? And then would the soccer team lose all their games because they couldn't get rainbow sparkle pedicures? And then would everyone be sad and mad, especially us?"

Aly rubbed Sparkly's head, thinking about it for a while. "Well," she said, "True Colors is older than you and it's older than me. No other salon has put it out of business yet, so I think it'll be okay."

"But Mom's still worried?" Brooke asked.

"Yeah," Aly said. "But Mom's still worried."

After Mom got off the phone, she, Aly, and Brooke made a dinner of macaroni and cheese—the kind that came from a box—and steamed broccoli. Then the three Tanner girls sat down to eat, and Sparkly lay down underneath the table to chew on a bone. Mom was very quiet and didn't even notice when Brooke took a second helping of macaroni before finishing her broccoli. That worried Aly.

"Mom," she said, after swallowing a broccoli stem, "you know True Colors is the best salon, right? And you have so many regulars who come every week and would never go anywhere else. You don't have to be nervous about Princess Polish or anything."

Mom put her fork down and sighed. "Thanks, Al," she said. "But I don't know if everyone would agree with you. I think I might start offering deals or special pedicures like Princess Polish."

Brooke reached for a third helping of macaroni. But this time, Mom raised an eyebrow at her, so Brooke sat back in her seat and dipped her broccoli in the leftover cheese instead. "What if you offer the same specials they do?" she asked. "Then it would be equal, so no one would have a reason to choose Princess Polish instead of True Colors."

Mom shook her head. "I don't want to start that kind of thing, because then I'm stuck offering whatever Princess Polish does. I want to come up with different promotions. Ideas that will make True Colors stand out."

Brooke chewed her cheesy broccoli. "What if you had a special deal for bridesmaids, like when Miss Lulu got married? Remember how many she had?"

"I do remember, Brookie," Mom said. "But I don't think enough people get married in our town each week to make that idea work."

Aly had slipped off her flip-flop and was petting Sparkly under the table with her toes. "The Sixth-Grade Fall Ball is a big deal," she said. "And we have some manicures and pedicures booked already. True Colors could have all Sparkle Spa's customers for the ball, if you want."

"That's a wonderful offer, sweetie," Mom answered, "but I think you should keep those customers. You've been working hard to build up your business. Just like I'm going to work hard to keep building mine. Don't worry, I'll think of something."

Everyone ate quietly for a little while.

Finally, Brooke asked, "What was it like at your Sixth-Grade Fall Ball, Mom?"

Mom took a sip of her water and smiled. "I didn't have a Sixth-Grade Fall Ball," she said. "But I did go to a Valentine's Day dance in sixth grade."

Aly tried to imagine what Mom looked like in sixth grade. She wondered if maybe Mom looked kind of like her. They did have the same hair, after all. And the same green eyes.

"What was it like?" Brooke asked, wiping another tree of broccoli through the last of the cheese on her plate. "Did you wear high heels? And have a sparkly pedicure?"

Putting her glass down and leaning back in her chair, Mom said, "It was a magical night. The gym was decorated with pink and red streamers, and there were hearts on all the walls. There was music, too, and candy and fruit punch."

"And you had high heels?" Brooke asked.

Mom shook her head. "No high heels. You know

how when we visit Grandma and Grandpa in the winter, there's always snow on the ground?"

Aly nodded. They usually visited their mother's parents in the summer, but the three times they'd gone in the winter, it was cold and snowy and Aly had to borrow Grandma's friend's daughter's old winter jacket.

"Well, it was snowing during the dance," Mom said, "and it was really cold. So we all had on boots. And tights and thick skirts and sweaters. I did have nail polish on, though. It was light pink, kind of like Kiss and Tell."

Brooke made a face. "Kiss and Tell is so light, it's barely even nail polish! And I can't believe you had to wear boots. I'm glad we live here, where we can wear flip-flops all the time. And no tights."

Aly laughed, but she wanted to hear the rest of Mom's story. "Why was it so magical?" she asked.

Mom smiled. "Do you know who I met at that sixth-grade dance?"

Aly shook her head, but Brooke said, "Joan?"

Joan was Mom's best friend and Aly and Brooke's very favorite True Colors manicurist, but Aly was pretty sure that Mom hadn't met her in sixth grade.

"Not Joan," Mom said with a laugh.

Aly wondered who it could be. "Was it a boy?" she asked.

Brooke's eyes popped open behind the bright blue frames of her glasses.

"I'll give you a clue," Mom said, smiling again. "He was tall and had wavy blond hair, and he was the smartest boy I'd ever met."

Aly felt like lightning had struck her brain. Their dad was tall and had wavy blond hair and was really, really smart. "Was his name Mark?" she asked excitedly.

Mom nodded her head, a grin on her face. "How'd you guess?"

"Wait," Brooke said. "Dad's name is Mark."

"It is," Mom said. "And I met him at a sixth-grade dance. He wasn't my boyfriend until much later, though."

Aly thought about the boys in her class. Was it possible that one day she'd marry one of them and have two daughters and her own nail salon? And was it possible that she'd meet him at the Fall Ball next year? So many cool things happened once you were a sixth grader. But first, she had to focus on getting through fifth grade and helping everyone going to this year's Fall Ball look their best. As long as her customers didn't decide to go to Princess Polish instead!

three

Candy Corn on the Cob

After school on Friday, Sparkle Spa wasn't that busy. It was so quiet that Aly's two best friends, Charlotte and Lily, and Brooke's best friend, Sophie, stayed there after their pedicures, flip-flops off, feet all pedicured.

"Thanks for suggesting Candy Corn on the Cob, Brooke," Sophie said, wiggling her toes in the drying area. "The gold sparkles make the yellow extra glittery."

"Can I keep experimenting on your toes, then?"

Brooke asked. "Because I have a new idea for the Fall Ball. We can do special pedicures with a stripe of a different sparkly color on the top part of the big toe. You know, like the toe is dipped in caramel or chocolate or something."

"Just the big toes?" Aly asked. "Not all of them?"

"Trust me," Brooke said, pulling I'm So Grapeful off the shelf.

"I trust you, Brooke," Sophie said.

Aly trusted her too. Brooke was a really talented artist, and somehow she seemed to know exactly which colors would look best together. Brooke was the one who had invented the soccer team's rainbow sparkle pedicure.

Brooke painted a medium-size stripe of glittery purple on top of the glittery yellow. The purple made the yellow look even brighter. It would've looked too wild if this combination was on every toe.

"You were right, Brookster," Aly said, inspecting Sophie's feet. "We should make that design the Fall Ball special pedicure."

"And you should make Candy Corn on the Cob the Color of the Week!" Lily was looking at last week's color, a glittery green called Hoppy Birthday.

"We do need a new one," Brooke said. "But maybe we should pick this coppery Autumn Princess instead."

"Nothing with the word 'princess'!" Aly groaned. "Princess Polish is already annoying enough!"

The phone rang in the main salon, and a few seconds later one of the manicurists, Jamie, came into Sparkle Spa. "Phone's for you, girls," she said, holding the cordless out toward Aly.

"Thanks, Jamie," Aly said, taking the phone. "Sparkle Spa," she said into the receiver. "How may I help you?"

The girl on the other end was talking really quickly.

"You want to *what*?" Aly asked—she hadn't quite heard the first time.

"Cancel," the girl said, more clearly now. "Cancel my appointment before the Fall Ball. I had it for noon next Saturday. I'm Uma."

Aly felt the blood drain from her face. She knew Uma from school, but not very well, and Uma had booked her appointment only yesterday.

"Can I ask why?" Aly said, even though the polite thing to do would've been just to say okay, remove her name from the appointment book, and forget about it.

"I changed my mind," Uma answered.

Aly imagined her shrugging on the other side of the phone.

"Okay," Aly said. "Thanks for letting us know."

She beeped off on the phone and erased Uma's name from the book.

"Did we lose a customer?" Brooke asked.

Aly nodded. "Not a regular. A sixth grader named Uma. I bet she's going to Princess Polish. She didn't say so, but still."

Brooke balled her hands into fists. "What are they doing to us? I *hate* Princess Polish."

"I'm not a fan either, Brookster," Aly said. "I think they may be taking some of our walk-ins, too."

Usually, by this point on a Friday afternoon, Aly and Brooke had customers who walked by, saw their sign, and came in for a pedicure or a manicure or both. But today Sparkle Spa was quiet. Aly guessed people saw the FREE PRINCESS PEDICURE! sign across the street and went there instead. She figured if she were someone who didn't know how cool Sparkle Spa was and she saw that sign, she might check out the new place too.

Brooke was tugging on her fishtail braid. Aly knew that meant her sister was nervous about Princess Polish and the missing customers.

"Hey, Aly, did you braid Brooke's hair today?" Lily asked. She was stringing beads at Sparkle Spa's jewelry-making area.

Aly nodded.

"Could you braid my hair like that? And maybe weave these beads into it?" She held up the thread she'd been stringing in a pattern of alternating silver, gold, and orange beads.

"Sure," Aly said. "Why not?" It wasn't like they had nails to polish.

"I like that style too," Sophie said. "Can you do that for me, Brooke?"

Brooke shook her head. "I can't do that kind of braid."

"I can!" Charlotte said. She got up from petting

Sparkly, who was asleep in his corner of the spa, behind a little gate.

"I'll string some beads," Brooke volunteered.

Aly and Charlotte began weaving the strings of beads into their friends' hair. Brooke found some ribbons to add as well. When the braids were finished, they looked beautiful.

"I just thought of something!" Brooke was so excited, she couldn't stand still. "Sparkle Spa can do sparkly braids. And we can do them for the Fall Ball! Princess Polish doesn't do hair. We'll get all our customers back!"

Sometimes Aly couldn't believe how smart Brooke was.

"I can be a braider," Charlotte offered. "I don't mind working for Sparkle Spa."

Aly thought this was a very good idea—the kind of idea they probably didn't even have to run past Mom.

Brooke ran to the supply closet near the back of the room and grabbed paper and a handful of markers. "Time to make a sign," she said.

While Lily kept stringing beads, Aly, Sophie, and Charlotte watched as Brooke drew the back of a girl's head, with a beautiful, sparkly beaded braid cascading down. Then she handed the marker to Aly. "You write the words," she said.

Aly thought for a moment and then wrote:

Sparkle Braids at Sparkle Spa!
Perfect for Auden's Sixth-Grade Fall Ball!
Call for an appointment!

She added the phone number for True Colors underneath.

Lily inspected the sign. "I think you should add 'Free' on there," she said. "People like free."

Aly looked at Brooke. Brooke looked back at Aly.

"We don't want to copy what Princess Polish does," Aly said. Actually, she kind of wished they could charge real money for this special service, like five or even ten dollars. Then they could give the money to True Colors.

Just then Aly had an idea—a Brooke sort of idea, but it was all her own. "Do you think," Aly started, "that maybe we could give the money in the donation jar to True Colors this time?"

"Yes, Aly," Brooke said. "That's the best idea!"

"But . . ." Sophie scratched her head. "But True Colors isn't a charity."

"But it *is* a place we love, and if Mom is losing business, it's a place that could use some help," Brooke reasoned. "Come on, let's write that on the poster!"

Aly wondered if Sophie was right, if maybe this wasn't her best idea ever and was something that would make Mom mad. But she picked up a marker and added to the bottom of the poster, in much smaller lettering:

All donations will go to True Colors.

Hopefully, Mom wouldn't mind. But just in case, Aly didn't push down very hard on the marker, so the writing wasn't very easy to see.

four

Apple Crispy

W hat are you girls doing?" Joan asked. She walked over to where Brooke was holding the poster to the window as Aly was taping it to the glass. Sophie, Charlotte, and Lily were outside, giving instructions on where to place the poster so that it would be most visible.

"Joanie Rigatoni Noodles!" Brooke said, turning her head. "We came up with a way to compete with Princess Polish. Aly and Charlotte are going to do beaded braids for the dance. Like mine. Look!"

33

She shook her head so Joan couldn't miss her sparkly braid.

"That's not a bad idea," Joan said, sitting down in an empty manicure chair. "We could use some more foot traffic in here. What did your mother think?"

Aly and Brooke gave each other a Secret Sister Eye Message: *Uh-oh, caught.*

"We haven't actually asked her yet," Aly said. "We looked for Mom before, while you were polishing Mrs. Bass's nails, but we didn't see her. And we figured this wasn't the kind of thing that needed her permission anyway. You know, it's a Sparkle Spa promotion."

Joan looked around the salon herself then, as though she doubted what Aly had said. But sure enough, only Lisa and Jamie were at the manicure stations, with Carla behind the welcome desk. And Emma was sitting all by herself in the waiting area, reading a magazine.

"Carla, do you know where Karen is?" Joan asked.

Carla stopped flipping through the appointment book to look up at Joan. "She said something about going to the print shop. To make coupons, I think."

Joan nodded. "I forgot she was doing that today." Then she turned to Brooke and Aly. "Well, I guess it's fine for you to braid hair in Sparkle Spa. I think I'm going to grab a coffee from Beans and Leaves. Carla can help you girls out if you need anything."

Only half an hour after the girls had hung their poster, Aly was braiding a customer's hair as quickly as she could—Charlotte, too—and there was a line of girls waiting to get their hair done. Not just sixth graders, either, and not just for a special occasion. Evidently, people liked getting their hair braided almost as much as they liked getting manicures and pedicures, for no particular reason at all!

Luckily, when Mom found out about the hair idea, she didn't argue. In fact, she thought it was a super plan.

Aly twisted a hair band around the bottom of a braid and sent her customer over to Sophie, who had gotten two mirrors—one from Carla and the other from Jamie—to show the girls what they looked like from behind once the style was completed. Sparkly was sitting next to Sophie and barked his approval every now and then.

The next girl in line sat down in front of Aly. Aly thought she recognized her from school.

"Hi," Aly said. "What color beads would you like in your braid?"

"Do you have red?" the girl asked.

"Brooke!" Aly called across the room. "Do we have red?"

Brooke inspected the strands of beads she and Lily had already made. "Red and gold!" she called back. "Kind of like Apple Crispy!"

"I like that," the girl in Aly's chair said. "I'm Daisy, by the way."

"Nice to meet you, Daisy. I'm Aly," Aly said. "And that's my sister, Brooke."

"I know who you guys are," Daisy said. "*Everyone* at school does."

This information was news to Aly. "Really?" she asked.

Daisy laughed. "How often do kids start a sparkly spa? You guys are famous."

Aly felt her face turn pink. "Um, anyway," she said, smiling, "do you want a French braid, Dutch braid, fishtail braid, backward braid, or regular braid?"

"Which one is the Dutch?" Daisy asked.

Aly pointed to one of the girls sitting in front of

Charlotte. "It's that one, where the braid kind of sits on top of your head."

"Okay, I'll go with that one," Daisy said. "I think it'll be a trial run for the Fall Ball."

Aly nodded and started the braiding, making sure every strand was even and straight as she wove in the beads. Aly thought it was the best braid she'd done so far. Braiding hair was kind of like polishing nails, she realized. The more you did it, the better you got.

Once Aly finished Daisy's hair and Daisy had checked herself out in the mirror, she asked to book an appointment before next weekend's ball. Within the hour, four other girls made Fall Ball appointments too—for braids *and* manicures and pedicures. They wanted the whole Sparkle Spa treatment!

Lily stood up and held the donation jar high in the air. It was a sparkly teal color, in the shape of a strawberry. Aly and Brooke's mom had made it back when she was in art school, before she owned a nail salon and became a mom.

"Don't forget to donate to the jar," Lily said. "We're giving all the money to True Colors!"

"Yay, True Colors!" Brooke cheered while stringing beads.

A few of the customers smiled, and Aly did too. Wait until Mom found out!

five

Pickle Me

Two days later, on Sunday morning, Dad was driving Aly and Brooke to the salon. Mom had gone in earlier to open up. Sparkly, who loved riding in the car, was standing on Brooke's lap with his nose out the window, sniffing the fresh air.

"So, Alligator," Dad said, looking in the rearview mirror at Aly. "Mom tells me this is the week you and your friends are decorating for the sixth-grade dance."

Aly nodded. With all the trouble because of Princess Polish, it had almost slipped her mind. "We are," she said. "Even though Brooke and I usually open Sparkle Spa on Fridays, we can't this week because that's the day the fifth graders are decorating the gym. The ball's on Saturday night."

"I wish I were a fifth grader," Brooke said, sighing. "Do you think I could pretend?"

Aly smiled at her sister. "I think people might notice that you're a little short for a fifth grader."

"What if I wore high heels?" Brooke asked hopefully. "Just a few inches?"

Dad shook his head. "You know the rules," he said quickly over his shoulder.

Brooke did know the rules. And Aly figured her sister didn't *really* believe that high heels would make her look that much older. But that was Brooke—she would try anything.

"Girls, I'll come get you around four," Dad said as he slowed to a stop in front of True Colors. "Mom's going to work late today. Maybe we can go to the movies tonight?"

"Can we get popcorn for dinner?" Brooke asked. "And Sno-Caps?"

Aly stopped herself from laughing out loud. She knew there was *no* way their dad was going to go for popcorn and chocolate as dinner.

"How about for dessert?" Dad said.

"Deal!" Brooke said. She popped the lock on her door, opened it right onto the sidewalk, and scooted out, with Aly and Sparkly following.

Aly couldn't help but steal a glance across the street at Princess Polish. She so wished they would just disappear into thin air. And she couldn't believe what she saw—a *new* sign was in their window:

PRINCESS HAIR DESIGN! BRAIDS! CURLS! UPDOS! BEADS!

FEATHERS! SPARKLES! TIARAS! WE HAVE IT ALL!

Under the words was a huge photograph of a girl

wearing a glittery crown with braids decorated with beads and feathers.

Aly felt like someone had kicked a soccer ball into her stomach. After Dad drove away, she quickly crossed the street so she could look inside the salon. She saw a few manicurists with high ponytails and matching pink aprons.

"What are you doing?" Brooke called out. "You know I can't cross without you!"

"Sorry, Brookie," Aly said, running back across the street to her sister. Then she pointed out the sign to Brooke.

"I can't even stand it!" Brooke shouted. "They copied our idea and made it even better. That's not fair."

Brooke stomped into True Colors and straight into Sparkle Spa without saying a word to anyone. Mom looked up at Aly and Sparkly, who were trailing behind.

"She saw the sign?" Mom asked from behind the welcome desk.

"We both did," Aly answered. "And we don't want to feel better about it. We just want to be mad for a while."

Mom nodded. "Okay. But just so you know, I'm mad too. You girls came up with a wonderful idea. I'm sorry they one-upped it."

"Me too," Aly said. And then she went into Sparkle Spa to be mad along with her sister.

When Clementine and Tuesday, two third graders who first came into Sparkle Spa during the pet adoption polish-a-thon Aly and Brooke had held, showed up for their manicures, Brooke was on the verge of tears. And when three different sixth graders called to cancel their Fall Ball hair-braiding appointments for next Saturday, she started crying.

After that, luckily (or unluckily), the salon was empty. Aly didn't think it would be great for business for customers to see one of the owners weeping.

"Don't worry, Brooke. We'll fix this," Aly assured her, and handed Brooke a cup of water. She wasn't really certain they could, but she wanted to make her sister feel better.

Aly realized she didn't feel sad, she felt mad. But she knew from dealing with mean Suzy Davis ever since kindergarten that being mad wouldn't change anything. It was time to do something to make the situation better. Anything at all.

"What if we make a list of ways to get more customers?" Aly said. "If we keep coming up with new ideas, maybe we can eventually wear Princess Polish down."

"But that's the *problem*," Brooke moaned. "They're idea stealers. Every idea we come up with, they'll just steal it and make it better. If they keep doing that, we might not even *have* Sparkle Spa for much longer."

"Then it's a good thing we're creative thinkers," Aly said. "Because we'll have to come up with *lots* of ideas. And maybe we'll come up with some they *can't* steal."

Aly went to the back of Sparkle Spa to get some pens and paper. She chose a blue pen for Brooke and a purple one for herself—one of her two favorite colors (the other was green), so maybe it would be lucky. She picked Sparkly up and put him on her lap. She thought that might be lucky too.

"Brooke, you face the door and I'll look at the wall. That way we don't distract each other. I'll set my watch and we'll brainstorm for five minutes. Okay?" Aly asked.

"Okay," Brooke answered, her blue marker uncapped and ready to write.

"Three, two, one, go," Aly said.

But just like the wall she was staring at, Aly's mind was blank. She kept hoping ideas would somehow magically appear. But when five minutes passed, Sparkly was asleep, Aly's paper was covered in purple hearts, and Brooke had drawn a picture of a puppy.

✳ ✳ ✳ ✳ ✳

Later there was a knock at the door. As Sparkly barked, Aly turned to see Charlotte with her twin brother, Caleb.

"Hi," Aly said. "Is your mom getting her nails done in True Colors?"

Charlotte nodded. "I figured maybe you could give me a new manicure? My polish from last time is starting to chip."

"Sure," Brooke said, standing up. "What color do you want?"

"I'll take a look," Charlotte said. "And Caleb wants his nails done too."

"No problem," Aly said, standing up next to Brooke. "Just cleaning and filing, like we did at the polish-a-thon?" she asked him.

Caleb stared at his shoes. Charlotte elbowed him. "Tell her!" she prodded.

Caleb kept staring at his shoes, but he said quietly, "Charlotte was telling me how rock stars get nail polish . . . and when we adopted Bob from Paws for Love, he had cool green nail polish. So, um, I was thinking maybe green?"

Brooke looked at Aly with raised eyebrows. Aly

returned the look and shrugged. "Sure, okay," she said to Caleb. "Why don't you pick out which green you want."

When Caleb and Charlotte walked over to the polish display, Brooke whispered to Aly, "I don't want to do a boy."

Aly sighed. "Boy hands are just the same as girl hands. And Mom and Joan and all the manicurists do men sometimes. But it's fine. I'll take Caleb. You do Charlotte."

Brooke nodded and walked over to one of the manicure stations to set up.

"Um, Aly?" Caleb asked. "Do you think Oscar the Green is a good one? Is that close to what you used on Bob?"

Aly joined Caleb at the display. "We used a different kind of polish on Bob, special for dogs," she said. "But that color's pretty close. So is this one." She picked up a bottle of Pickle Me and handed it to him.

"I like this one better," Caleb said. "Thanks, Aly."

He smiled at her, and then he looked down at his shoes again. Aly looked at his shoes too, to see what was so interesting down there, but all she saw were dirty sneakers with double-knotted laces.

Aly sat down across from Caleb and started cleaning his nails.

Charlotte had chosen Strawberry Sunday and was sitting across from Brooke, who was taking off Charlotte's old polish.

"Aly," Charlotte said, "did you sign up for a job on the decorating committee yet? Caleb and I signed up for balloons."

Aly had been in such a hurry to get to Sparkle Spa after school on Friday, she'd forgotten to sign up. She shook her head. "I didn't. But I can see if there's still an opening for balloons tomorrow."

"I think balloons is the best job," Caleb said, "because you get to use the helium tank."

"When I'm a fifth grader, I'm going to sign up

for posters," Brooke said. She was filing Charlotte's right-hand nails while Charlotte's left hand was soaking in warm, sudsy water.

"Who do you think is going to get the On the Ball trophies?" Charlotte asked.

"Well, Jenica started the after-school sports program, and Lucas Grant made up that kindergarten reading program, so I think it should be the two of them," Aly said. "Or I hope so, at least. What about you, Caleb?"

Caleb shrugged but managed to keep his left hand steady. Aly was impressed. "I don't really know many of the sixth graders," he said. "But next year I bet it'll be you. For doing things like the polish-a-thon to help raise money for dog adoptions and stuff."

Aly felt her face turning really hot, and she knew her cheeks must be the color of Pink Lemonade Float. "Thanks," she said.

"Aly?" Caleb said once she was finished cleaning

his nails. "I think I want Pickle Me only on my thumbs. I think it'll look cooler that way."

"What a cool idea, Caleb," Brooke said. "We can call it the 'thumbs-up manicure'!"

Caleb grinned at Brooke. After a few more minutes Charlotte's and Caleb's nails were done and dry, and their mom poked her head into Sparkle Spa to get them.

"See you at school tomorrow," Charlotte said, dropping some money in the donation jar.

"Yeah, see you," Caleb said. "And thanks for my rock star nails—I mean thumbs." He scratched Sparkly behind the ears and gave a thumbs-up sign to Brooke and Aly.

"You're welcome," Aly said. "Come back whenever you want."

Brooke pulled out the girls' doodle-covered lists from before. "Okay," she said, "let's start thinking about how to get more customers. For real this time."

Aly stared at the paper and then said, "Before we start again, I'm going to take Sparkly for a walk."

Aly and Sparkly walked past Beans and Leaves and A Taste of Chocolate. She stopped in front of John's Sport Shop, looking at the soccer balls, baseball bats, and lacrosse sticks. And just like that, she got an idea.

"Come on, puppy. Let's run back to the salon." The two of them raced down the sidewalk.

"Boys!" Aly said when she rushed through the Sparkle Spa door. "We need to get more boys!"

Brooke wrinkled her nose. "But boys mostly don't like sparkles."

"But Caleb liked Pickle Me," Aly reminded her. "And we can tell them that even if they don't want rock star thumbs like his, they should still have clean nails for the Fall Ball! I mean, if dogs can get their nails done, so can boys."

Brooke pushed her glasses up higher on her nose. "I guess it's not the worst idea. But I'm still going to think of some more."

Just then Sparkly started whining as Joan walked into the back room carrying a large flat box and a brown paper bag. "Pizza Picnic time!" she announced to the girls. "I made some cookies for you to try, too."

Aly smiled. She loved Sunday Pizza Picnics with Joan. Her cookies were the best anywhere. Sometimes people even paid her to make cookies for weddings, birthdays, or fancy parties. "Great," Aly said, getting up to go grab their picnic blanket.

"We're trying to make another list of ways to get more customers," Brooke told Joan once the blanket was on the floor and they were eating. "But we only came up with one idea so far. Actually, it's Aly's idea. It's to get more boys to come."

Joan stopped eating mid-bite. Then she swallowed.

"That's actually an excellent idea, Aly." Joan got up from her spot and stuck her head into True Colors. "Karen, come in here for a sec," she called.

"What is it?" Mom asked. She took a seat next to Aly on the blanket.

"Aly has an idea for a special promotion for boys in Sparkle Spa. I think it might work in True Colors, too."

"Even if they don't want their nails polished, we can try to get them to have clean fingers," Aly explained.

"We can call them *man*-icures!" Brooke said with a laugh.

Mom smiled. A genuine big smile. "Fantastic!" she said. "Joan, when you and the girls are done with your pizza, let's figure out a plan. Princess Polish won't know what hit 'em."

Six
Midnight Blues

On Monday, Aly made sure to find Jenica before the first bell. She told her the boy plan for Sparkle Spa. Jenica loved it. "I'll spread the word," she said. "Don't worry, we'll have your salon filled with guys in no time. Man-icures it is."

By recess, Aly couldn't believe how quickly Jenica and her friends had relayed the message. Everyone at Auden Elementary knew about the man-icures. Some sixth-grade boys wouldn't set foot in anything that had the word "sparkle" in it, but three of them came up to Aly at recess, asking for appointments. They started with "Jenica told me . . ." or "Mia told me . . ." or "Anjuli told me . . . ," and they finished by asking about a "thumbs-up man-icure," stressing the "man" part.

Aly was standing against the fence that surrounded the soccer field, talking to Charlotte and Lily, when Lucas walked up to her.

"You're Aly, right?" he said.

Aly nodded. But she couldn't squeak out any words.

"So Jenica told me," he said, "that all guys should get man-icures for the ball. So I was thinking maybe I should book one."

Aly nodded again.

Then Lily elbowed her, which seemed to fix whatever had happened to her mouth.

"Okay," Aly said. "That'd be great." She pulled

the little Sparkle Spa appointment book out of the pocket of her jean shorts—the one that she brought to school so she could transfer appointments into the bigger one later—and opened it up. "Do you want the special thumbs-up man-icure or just a regular man-icure?"

"Thumbs-up means a color?" Lucas asked.

"Yes," Aly said. "Like black or green or gold or blue or really anything you want. Just on your thumbs, though."

Lucas looked down at his fingers, then back up at Aly. "I think just regular," he said. "No offense, I've just never had polish on my fingernails, you know?"

"Sure," Aly said, even though she wanted to explain to him that Caleb had looked really cool with his thumbs-up man-icure. "How's Saturday at one thirty?"

"That works for me." Lucas put his hand out to

shake Aly's. She stuck her pen in her pocket and stuck her hand out too. She couldn't believe she was actually touching Cute Lucas's skin.

"See you Saturday," Lucas said. And then he left to go join a soccer game on the field.

"Oh my gosh, Cute Lucas is coming!" Charlotte said. "I'm so glad I'm braiding hair so I can see him there."

"I think maybe I have to come in and string some more beads," Lily said. "You need more, right?"

Aly laughed. "Absolutely," she said.

After Lucas made his appointment, two more sixth-grade boys came by asking about man-icures, followed by a couple of fifth graders.

"I know I'm not going to the dance," said Garrett, who sat next to Aly in class, "but I want a man-icure anyway—one like Caleb's."

Cameron, who was also in Aly's class, made a face, but Caleb high-fived Garrett while Aly opened her appointment book again. "No problem," she said. "Let's pick a time."

By the end of the school day, Aly was thrilled with the success of the man-icure promotion—at least seven boys were coming. A few girls had booked nail appointments too, along with sparkle braids. Even though Sparkle Spa was closed on Mondays, Aly asked Brooke if she wanted to stop by True Colors to tell Mom about all the appointments and new customers.

"Definitely," Brooke said. "And then we can get Sparkly from the salon and take him to the park."

The two girls took their usual route from school to True Colors, walking slowly, not worrying about how long it took them to get there. The sun was shining, they had tons of customers, and nothing could ruin their happy mood. Not even Princess Polish.

When they got to the salon, they saw a couple of

new signs in the window. One was for man-icures. In midnight blue lettering, the sign read:

> A man's hands work hard all day.
> Take care of them with a man-icure
> engineered especially for men,
> offered at a discount!

Mom had added a hand-drawn illustration to the poster. The girls had only recently learned how good an artist their mother was, and Aly was amazed by how realistic the hands looked.

Next to the man-icure poster was another one that Aly and Brooke weren't expecting:

> After a long day at school,
> your feet need a break!
> special half-price pedicures
> for teachers!

On this poster, Mom had drawn feet at the bottom and decorated the border with images of math equations, alphabet letters, an apple, a ruler, and various other school supplies.

Aly stopped in her tracks. "Brooke, do you see what I see?" she asked.

"The half-price offer for teachers?" Brooke asked back.

"Yes," Aly said, looking away from the sign and over at her sister.

"Does that mean . . . Mrs. Fishman?" Brooke asked in horror. Mrs. Fishman was Brooke's third-grade teacher. She and Brooke didn't get along very well. Well, they got along fine when Brooke stopped jabbering all day long, but that didn't happen too often.

Aly nodded. "I think it could. And Mrs. Glass and Mrs. Roberts."

Brooke's eyes were enormous behind her glasses.

"If all those teachers come in and we have to see their bare feet . . . I don't think I can do this."

Aly felt the same way as Brooke—teachers should stay in school. They shouldn't become customers of your mother's nail salon. But then Aly glanced back across the street at Princess Polish.

"It's for business, I guess," Aly said.

Brooke shook her head. "Teacher feet! What's next?"

Aly laughed. "I don't know, Brookster. Principal Rogers's toes?"

Princess Polish was making their lives more interesting, that was for sure.

seven
Plum Delicious

The girls opened Sparkle Spa on Tuesday and Thursday that week—taking care of as many advance Fall Ball appointments as they could before Saturday's rush—so on Friday afternoon, Aly was free to focus on decorating the school gym for the dance.

"I'm *soooo* excited," Charlotte said as she and Lily walked down the hall with Aly. "Did you sign up for balloons, Lily?"

"I did," Lily said.

When the girls got to the gym, they checked in

with Miss Gonzales, who was the newest sixth-grade teacher and was in charge of the dance. "Balloons are in the back corner, girls," she said, looking at the list on her clipboard. Then she added, "Can you please tie the ribbons on for the boys? They're over by the helium tank."

"But—" Lily began.

Aly gave her a look that said, *Shush.* "No problem," she told Miss Gonzales.

"We'll ask the boys to switch later," she whispered to Lily. "Don't worry."

As the girls walked through the gym, they couldn't believe how busy it was everywhere.

One group of fifth graders was coloring posters with glitter markers. Another was laying out tablecloths on the folding tables and sprinkling glitter on top. There were kids twisting purple and gold streamers—Auden's colors—and handing them to teachers who were up on ladders, attaching them to walls and rafters. The gym was definitely starting to look less like a place for PE and more like a place where people would wear fancy clothes and beads in their hair.

Caleb and Garrett were filling balloons with helium, then handing them to Daniel and Bennett, who knotted them closed.

Aly, Charlotte, and Lily took the balloons and tied long purple and gold ribbons to each one. They started chatting as they worked.

"Are we all set with customers tomorrow?" Charlotte asked. "I'm still doing braids, right?"

Aly nodded. "Absolutely. I think it will be crowded . . . though the schedule isn't completely filled yet."

Aly was disappointed that some of the girls from the soccer team—Bethany, Maxie, Valentina, and Joelle—hadn't signed up for appointments. It could mean that they weren't going to the ball or that they just didn't want to get their hair or nails done, but Aly suspected it meant they'd chosen to go to Princess Polish instead. It wouldn't be so bad if sixth graders Aly didn't know very well did that, but it upset her to think some of her regulars might.

"It's okay, Aly," Charlotte said, seeming to read her thoughts. "We don't need *all* the sixth-grade girls who are going to the ball there. We just need enough of them to keep us busy all day."

"And enough so that we make money to help out True Colors," Aly said, because that was really the point of this. "As long as my mom agrees to take it, that is. It's going to be a big surprise."

"We're going to make so much money," Lily said as she tied a golden string tightly to the bottom of a balloon. "I can help too, right?"

"You can be the organizer and donations collector," Aly said. During the polish-a-thon that raised

money for Paws for Love, Aly and Brooke had orga-
nizers, and it had really helped the day go smoothly.
"You can make sure everyone knows when their
appointments are and remind them to make a donation before they leave. And you can keep an eye on
the boys so they don't get too . . . boyish."

Lily laughed. "I'll make sure to tell them about
the suggested donation of three dollars. I'll keep saying it, so everyone really understands." She and Aly
had come up with the idea of suggested donation
amounts during lunch that day, figuring it would be
a good way to guide customers toward fair donations
for True Colors.

Lily tied another ribbon to another balloon and
then let it float up to join all the others they'd already
finished. The ceiling was starting to look really cool,
with the lights shining through the balloons casting
purple and gold spots all over the gym floor. "Do you

think we can trade places with the boys at the helium tank now?"

Charlotte nodded. Lily went to talk to Caleb and the rest of the boys, who had started playing keep-away with a purple balloon. Mr. Mehta, the music teacher, who was in charge of the helium tank, didn't look too happy.

But the person walking toward them looked *really* happy. It was Aly's least favorite person in the whole school: Suzy Davis. She'd been mean for as long as Aly could remember, and she'd been especially mean to Aly since Sparkle Spa had opened.

"Hey, Aly," Suzy said, holding a box of markers and smiling the biggest smile Aly had ever seen on her. "So I heard Princess Polish is taking all your customers. I mean, I understand why. Who would want to come to your silly little back room when they can go to a real, grown-up spa and be treated like a princess? For free."

Aly swallowed. Whenever Suzy said something like that to her, Aly didn't know how to respond. Mostly because what Suzy said always sounded like it might be true. Who *would* want to come to Sparkle Spa when there was a real spa that welcomed kids right across the street?

Charlotte walked a few steps closer to Aly and snapped a knot in a Plum Delicious–colored balloon. "For your information," she said to Suzy, "Sparkle Spa has a packed schedule tomorrow. And *I'm* braiding hair."

"Well, Heather and I," Suzy said, "are going to Princess Polish to get ready for our parents' anniversary party. I'm sure that their braiders are better than you."

Aly clenched her fists. Insulting Sparkle Spa was one thing, but insulting Charlotte was something else altogether. "Charlotte is the best hair braider around,"

Aly said. "I bet she could braid circles around any of the grown-ups at Princess Polish."

Charlotte and Aly were standing shoulder to shoulder now, staring at Suzy.

"Whatever," Suzy said. "Sparkle Spa will always be for babies." Then she marched off in the direction of the poster team.

"She is the pits," Charlotte said, rubbing the balloon she was holding across her head to make her hair all staticky.

"The absolute pits," Aly agreed, even though she couldn't help feeling that Suzy was a little bit right.

Aly looked around at the transformed gym. Tomorrow night the sixth graders would be having the best time ever, and hopefully Sparkle Spa would have something to do with that—no matter what Suzy Davis thought.

eight
Very Ice Try

Aly felt a thud on her chest and then a lick on her cheek.

"Stop, Sparkly," she giggled. But Sparkly kept licking until Aly got out of bed.

It was just as well that Sparkly woke Aly up early, though, because today was the day of the Fall Ball.

Aly got dressed quickly and took Sparkly out for a walk. By the time they got back, Brooke was sitting at the kitchen table, ready to go.

"I'm so excited, it's almost like we're going to the ball ourselves," Brooke said on the drive to True Colors.

But Aly shook her head. "I think it's more like we're the fairy godmothers and all our customers are Cinderella."

Brooke laughed. But then she got serious. "Remember, I'm not doing boy feet."

"I don't think we have any boys scheduled for pedicures," Aly said after swallowing a bite of her granola bar. "Just for cleanings and thumbs-up man-icures."

"Ew," Brooke said. "That means their feet will be even grosser. It's a good thing fancy boy shoes cover up their toes."

Aly and Mom laughed. "Brooke, I don't know where you come up with that stuff," Mom said. Brooke just shrugged and laughed a little herself.

* * * * *

Once they got to Sparkle Spa, the sisters set out all the fall-themed polishes on a special table. Brooke also drew the shape of a foot on a piece of paper. Then Aly polished the toenails with Brooke's special "caramel-dipped pedicure" so everyone could see what it would look like. And she pulled out the strands of multicolored beads Brooke and Sophie had strung all week. There were dozens of them in at least eight different colors, and Brooke had organized them in rainbow order. They looked beautiful all by themselves, but they were going to look even nicer in people's hair.

By ten thirty, the girls were ready for the big day ahead, and Jenica was the first customer to arrive. She was carrying a royal-blue dress with spaghetti straps and ruffles. "I brought my dress to make sure the polish matched," she said. "I'd hate to get home and find that the polish clashed with this color."

Brooke had a very serious expression on her face. "You'd never want that," she said, tugging on her braid. "What color are your sandals again?"

"Silver," Jenica answered.

Brooke nodded. "Aly can start on your hair. I'll bring you different color choices for your nails."

Once Jenica sat down, Aly asked, "Silver beads to go with your shoes? Or blue?"

"Silver!" Brooke called from the polish display.

Aly smiled and raised an eyebrow at Jenica.

"Silver," Jenica confirmed. "And can you do that kind of braid that goes across my head? Like a crown?"

"Sure," she said, picking up a strand of silver beads to start.

Meanwhile, Brooke came back holding a bottle of silvery Very Ice Try and a bottle of hot-pink I Like to Mauve It Mauve It. "Here's what I'm thinking," she said. "Pink looks really good with bright blue, so I can use mauve on your toenails and then a stripe of silver on your big toes. And then we could do the opposite for your fingernails—silver with a stripe of pink."

"Will that be too much silver on her toes, since her sandals are silver?" Aly asked as Jenica's silky hair slid through her fingers.

Brooke ran back over to the display. She returned with Good Knight, which was almost the exact color of Jenica's blue dress. "Pink with a blue stripe on her toes. Then silver polish with a pink stripe on her fingers."

"Love it," Jenica said, and gave Brooke a high five.

Aly tucked the ends of Jenica's braid underneath the braid itself and lifted up a hand mirror. "What do you think?" she asked.

Jenica breathed out slowly. "Wow, Aly, I hardly

recognize myself. Thank you." She gave Aly a big smile before she followed Brooke to a pedicure chair.

As soon as Brooke began working on Jenica's toes, the rest of the Auden Angels soccer players started flowing in for their appointments. Just like Jenica, a lot of the sixth graders had brought along their dresses to make sure the polish they picked would look good with their outfits.

- Anjuli's dress was bright purple.
- Giovanna's was light pink.
- Mia was wearing orange.
- Avery, emerald green.
- Aubrey, mint green.

It was so busy for the next few hours that Aly really didn't have time to think about Princess Polish once. Okay, maybe once. All but four of the sixth-grade team members were there—Bethany, Joelle, Maxie, and Valentina—and Aly tried not to let that bother her, but it was kind of hard.

"My mom is letting me wear lip gloss," she heard Mia tell Giovanna. "Actually, it's more like tinted ChapStick. But it makes my lips a little pink."

Giovanna sighed. "I'm not even allowed to wear that. Just clear ChapStick. It's so not fair."

"But do you get to wear heels?" Brooke asked.

"Little ones," Giovanna said, showing Brooke the height with her thumb and pointer finger—about half an inch, Aly figured.

Aly had just finished painting Aubrey's fingers Candy Corn on the Cob with a crown of Very Ice Try on the thumbs when she looked up and saw Lucas Grant standing in the doorway, right on time. Her breath caught in her throat.

Cute Lucas! At Sparkle Spa! And she was going

to do his nails! She'd known it was going to happen, but it still caught her off guard. She had to remind herself to breathe. And to talk.

"Come on in, Lucas," she said. Only her voice sounded more like a croak than real words. His friend Oliver was behind him. "You too, Oliver," Aly added. They were the first two boys scheduled.

They walked in slowly—like they weren't sure they really wanted to do this—and the minute they entered, all the girls stopped chattering.

It was the quietest Sparkle Spa had ever been.

"Um, hi," Lucas said.

Every one of the girls—in the manicure chairs, in the pedicure chairs, and at the braiding stations—stared at the boys.

Was this a mistake? Aly wondered. Were the man-icures a bad idea?

The air seemed so thick that Aly felt like she would

need nail clippers to cut it. She took a deep breath.

"I think it's so neat that you guys are here," Mia finally said from where Charlotte was braiding her hair. "Right, Giovanna?" she asked.

Giovanna nodded. "Definitely," she said. "Extra cool."

Aly saw Oliver smile. Maybe this was going to be okay after all.

Lily looked at the appointment book. "Lucas, you're first," she said. "You can go over there with Aly. Oliver, you're welcome to wait in the corner on the pillows until he's done. Then Aly will do your nails."

Oliver plopped himself down next to Aubrey, whose nails were drying. Lucas sat across from Aly.

"Hey," he said.

"Hey," Aly said back, suddenly very aware that she was touching a boy's fingers. A really cute boy's fingers.

But Lucas didn't seem to notice how awkward she felt. He just smiled so that a dimple appeared on his left cheek.

Aly smiled too. When she was done with his nails, Lucas looked at his fingers and grinned. "My hands look like my dad's now," he said. "Like, important. Nice job."

Then he jammed his hands in his jeans pockets and traded seats with Oliver.

As Aly started cleaning Oliver's nails, some more girls came in, and then Garrett and Caleb, even though they weren't going to the dance.

Mom poked her head in and winked at Aly. Aly winked back. It was kind of like a Secret Sister Eye Message, except it was with her mother instead of her sister. The wink clearly meant: *Princess Polish is not going to stop Sparkle Spa!*

"Aly," Garrett shouted across the room. "What's

the best rock star nail polish color for my thumbs-up man-icure?"

"I'll help him, Aly," Brooke said, walking Giovanna to the drying area.

Brooke pushed her glasses up against her nose. "Well," she said, "I like Guitar-ange a lot, but you have gray eyes, so you might like Heavy Metal or—"

But before Brooke could finish, Bethany, Maxie, and Joelle raced into Sparkle Spa. "HELP! You have to help! Look at what Princess Polish did to us!"

nine

Heavy Metal

What happened? Let me see!" Brooke ran over and took Bethany's hand in hers. It was terrible. The polish, which looked like it had started out pink, was turning into a weird orangey yellow at the edges and peeling away from Bethany's fingernails.

Aly could see tears in Bethany's eyes. "We were done about an hour ago," she sniffed. "And then we all went home, and next thing I knew, I looked at my hands, and *this* had happened. And then I called

Maxie and Joelle and found out their polish was doing the same thing. Valentina's, too, but her mom's trying to fix it at home."

Maxie held out her hands. Her blue nails were peeling and turning green. Joelle's red nails were peeling and turning orange.

Aly pulled Joelle's hand closer and inspected the polish. "I think it's old," she said. "Like, really old. Maybe the stuff that makes the polish work like normal went bad."

"Can you fix it?" Joelle asked. "Please? We never should have gone to Princess Polish, right, guys? We're sorry."

Bethany nodded.

"We're so, *so* sorry," Maxie added. "We just . . . we thought it would be neat to go to a grown-up salon. But Sparkle Spa is so much better."

Aly heard what Maxie said, and she kind of

understood it, but before she could answer, she was distracted by a purple splotch on Maxie's forehead, just under a purple feather that was woven into her hair. She looked at the rest of the purple feathers in Maxie's hair. Every single spot where a feather touched her skin, Maxie had a purple splotch—on her neck, her ears, and her forehead.

"Um," Aly said, "I think your feathers are turning your skin purple."

"What?" Maxie ran to a full-length mirror on the closet door and screamed. She turned back to Aly. "You *have* to fix it. All of it!"

Maxie's scream brought Mom running, with Miss Gonzales, the sixth-grade teacher from Auden, behind her. Miss Gonzales put down the bag she was carrying and hurried over to Maxie. "What's wrong?" she asked, just as Mom said, "Is everything okay in here?"

"Take a look for yourself," Aly said. "Princess Polish bought cheap feathers, and now Maxie's turning purple."

"Let me see," Miss Gonzales said, inspecting Maxie's forehead. Maxie tilted her head closer to the teacher. "I think you can get it off with soap and water. It'll be fine. You'll still look lovely tonight."

As Miss Gonzales and Mom returned to True Colors, Maxie pleaded, "Can you get me back to normal, Aly? Please, please, please?"

Brooke stared at Aly over her glasses, sending the Secret Sister Eye Message: *I am still very mad at them.* But Aly shook her head at Brooke. What kind of people would they be if they let Bethany and Maxie and Joelle go to the Fall Ball with messed-up nails and color-splotched skin? They were more professional than that.

"We can do it," Aly answered. "But you'll have to

wait. We have other customers with booked appointments," and she pointed to the group of boys now waiting at the door.

"That's right." Brooke nodded. "You'll have to wait."

Aly handed cotton balls and polish remover to Maxie, Joelle, and Bethany. "And you'll have to help out," she added.

But the girls weren't looking at Aly, they were staring at all the boys in Sparkle Spa.

"What happened to you three?" a lacrosse player named Aiden asked.

"Don't look!" Bethany squealed as she turned around and tried to hide her face in her arm.

Maxie covered her face with her arm too. "Ack! I can't believe that the one day I have purple spots on my face is the same day that *boys* are at Sparkle Spa."

Joelle stood her ground. "We had a feather problem," she told the boys. "But it's going to be fixed." Then she turned to Aly and said, "Thank you for fixing us."

"Thank you," Bethany echoed. "So much. We'll never go anywhere else to get our nails done again."

"Never," Maxie agreed, her face still in her arm.

The boys looked at one another. "Did she say 'feathers'?" asked Lee, who played the trumpet in the band with Lucas.

"She did," Lucas confirmed from the spot where he was waiting for Oliver. "But don't worry. They don't do feathers in here. You're safe."

Aly couldn't help but laugh. Then she returned her attention to Oliver's man-icure.

"This place is crazy!" he said to her as she finished filing his nails.

Aly nodded. "Today for sure," she said. "It's a good thing our dog is home with our dad."

"Sometimes there's a dog in here too?" Oliver asked.

"A little one," Aly said. "Okay, I think you're all done now."

Oliver held up his hands and inspected them. "My hands do look kind of different. My nails are, like, smooth and shiny. Thanks, Aly."

Aly smiled. "Well, you're welcome to come back whenever you want."

Oliver called out to Lucas, and just as they left another sixth-grade girl burst through the door. She had green feathers in her hair and green splotches on her skin. Aly knew what she was going to say before she opened her mouth.

"Do you need us to fix you up before the Fall Ball?" she asked.

The girl nodded.

Aly ran her fingers through her hair. "Okay, just

go talk to Lily—she'll schedule you in." She pointed the girl in Lily's direction.

Soon after that, two more sixth graders came in with the same Princess Polish problems. And just when Aly thought there couldn't be any more surprises, the biggest one of the day walked through the door.

Suzy Davis.

Followed by her younger sister, Heather.

"What are you doing here?" Brooke asked.

They rushed past Brooke, right over to Aly. Suzy stared at the floor, and she spoke so softly, Aly could barely hear her.

"Tonight's my parents' anniversary party, and Heather and I went to Princess Polish. I don't know what happened, but our nails are peeling and turning colors, and Princess Polish won't do anything about it. I know Sparkle Spa isn't as fancy as they are, but, um, I was wondering if maybe you could, um . . . Ugh!" Suzy looked up. "Could you help us?"

Aly thought about all the awful things Suzy Davis had said and done at school over the years. If Aly started from kindergarten, she could probably count up to a hundred. That gave her an idea. One of her better ones, she thought.

"We'll help," she said, "but you have to make me a deal. If we redo your nails, you can't say anything mean to me for the rest of the school year."

"Mean? Who's mean?" Suzy said. Then she rolled her eyes. "Fine, Aly. Whatever. Deal. You just have to fix us."

Deal? Aly couldn't believe Suzy had agreed.

"Okay, then," Aly said. Honestly, she would've fixed Heather's nails anyway, and maybe even Suzy's, but this was fantastic. She wondered if Suzy would keep up her end of the bargain and actually leave her alone at school now. It would be fun to see.

Aly directed Suzy and Heather over to the waiting area, handing them some cotton balls and polish remover to give them a head start. Then she sat down at her manicure station across from Garrett.

"Did Suzy Davis just promise to be nice to you?" he whispered, handing her a bottle of Heavy Metal for his thumbs-up man-icure.

"Yes," Aly said as she dunked his hands in warm, soapy water.

"Is it always this weird in Sparkle Spa?" he asked.

Aly laughed. "No," she said. "Today seems extra weird."

But it was also extra exciting.

Aly looked around the salon. Brooke was giving one pedicure after another, and Charlotte was furiously unbraiding and rebraiding hair. And the bracelet-making area was filled with waiting customers.

Aly and Brooke were grinning from ear to ear as they sent each other one of their silent messages: *This is one of the most sparkly days ever!*

ten

News Prince

Three hours later Sparkle Spa was empty. Only Brooke and Aly were left, sitting in the pedicure chairs, hardly able to move. All their customers were gone, and Charlotte's mom had just picked her and Lily up to take them home.

"*That* was the craziest day ever," Brooke said, flopping back against the seat cushion. "Since it's Saturday, I'd say it's time for us to do each other's nails. I'd been thinking News Prince because of the extra glitter, but maybe tomorrow. I'm all polished out."

Aly flopped against her own chair. "I'm all polished out too. And braided out. And talked out. And everything-ed out."

"Everything-ed out," Brooke repeated with a sigh. "That's totally it. I'm everything-ed out. But at least everyone will look beautiful at the Fall Ball. I know you said before that we'd be like fairy godmothers today, but I think it's more like we were Cinderella's mice, racing around all day. No wicked stepsisters, no carriage turning into a pumpkin at the stroke of midnight . . . but everyone really will look like princesses."

"Or princes," Aly added, looking around the room and noticing how much straightening up they had to do. She slowly got up and started putting polish bottles back in the display.

"You know, Brooke, I wish we could see the whole thing—everyone all dressed up, the party lights, the dancing, the fancy food . . ."

"Me too," Brooke said. "Actually, I could use

some fancy food myself right now. Maybe we can clean up later?"

"Food would be good," Aly said. "But let's bring Mom the money from the donation jar first—make sure she'll take it for True Colors so all our work will have been worth it. Can you believe we've been able to keep this a secret from her for so long?"

Before Aly even finished her sentence, Brooke was already heading into the main salon. Aly grabbed the donation jar and followed.

Everyone had left True Colors except for Mom, who was at the reception desk, going through the day's receipts; Joan, who was cleaning up her manicure station; and Mrs. Franklin, one of the girls' favorite regulars, who was zipping up her purse and heading out the door.

"Joanie," Brooke said, "do you have any cookies today? Aly and I are Starvin' Marvins."

Joan tucked some hair back into Brooke's braid.

"Sorry," she said. "I didn't have a chance to bake last night."

Mom looked up from the reception desk and checked her watch. Aly checked hers too: 5:52. "I just have a few more things to do," Mom said, but then she noticed that Aly was holding the Sparkle Spa donation jar. "Why are you carrying the jar, Aly?"

"Mom," Aly began, waving Brooke to her side. "We've decided to give True Colors our donations. We didn't count it, but it looks like a lot."

"Oh, girls," Mom said. She looked like she was about to cry.

Brooke added, "There's a lot more money in there than usual, not only because of all our extra customers for the Fall Ball, but because we came up with suggested donations for our special services today. Please take it. We want you to have it all—to help keep True Colors open."

"Plus," Aly said, "if it weren't for True Colors, there wouldn't be a Sparkle Spa. And we don't want Princess Polish to put both of us out of business."

Mom didn't say a word. Aly couldn't tell if she was angry or happy.

After what seemed like forever, she finally said, "You girls amaze me. But as kind and generous and thoughtful as you are, I can't accept your donation."

"But why not?" asked Brooke. "We did this for you." Now it looked as though Brooke might cry.

Mom pulled Aly and Brooke close and kissed the tops of their heads. "True Colors isn't a charity. And while I'm not happy that Princess Polish has moved in across the street, my business is doing fine. You don't have to worry. But I love you girls more than I can say for caring as much as you do. We'll figure out a different charity to donate the money to—maybe Businesswomen Unite this time? It's a charity that helps women entrepreneurs start their own businesses."

Mom hugged both of the girls again. "How does that sound?" she asked.

"If you think that's best," Aly said. And then her stomach chose that time to rumble.

"You two really are hungry, aren't you?" Mom asked.

Aly was, actually, very hungry. She hadn't eaten lunch today.

"We are!" Brooke answered.

"Why don't you let them run out and grab something from the Sweetery, Karen?" Joan suggested.

Mom pulled a few bills out of her wallet. "That's a good idea," she said. "Here's ten dollars. While you're at the bakery, Joan and I will start cleaning up Sparkle Spa for you."

"You don't have to do that, Mom," Aly said. She

wanted to show her mother she and Brooke were responsible business owners, which meant cleaning up after themselves.

Mom squeezed her shoulder. "Don't worry about it," she said. "But don't get used to it either." And she winked.

"Wow! I haven't been outside all day," Brooke said once the sisters left True Colors. "The fresh air feels good. . . . I think I'm going to get something chocolatey with sprink—" Brooke stopped mid-sentence and tugged on Aly's sleeve. "Look, Aly." She pointed across the street.

Princess Polish was dark. The lights were out.

"It looks like they closed early," Brooke said.

Aly squinted. "I think there's a sign on the door."

The girls walked to the corner and crossed the street to check it out.

CLOSED FOR AN EMERGENCY, the sign read.

"Do you think they *really* had an emergency?" Brooke asked.

Aly shook her head. "Not a real one. I think they used old polish and cheap feathers and ended up with a lot of unhappy customers."

Brooke nodded. "Do you think they'll close for good?"

Aly looked at the sign and peered in through the window. "I don't know," she answered. "Maybe it's temporary, until they get new supplies."

"Well, I hope it's for good." Brooke slipped her hand into Aly's as they kept walking toward the bakery.

"Me too," Aly said. "And I hope no other nail salons open up nearby."

"Just True Colors and Sparkle Spa," Brooke said.

It was funny, though. Aly was thinking that having Princess Polish there did make Sparkle Spa better—it had made them come up with some new ideas, which was always a good thing.

The bells from the church downtown started to ring. Aly counted the bongs. One, two, three, four, five, six.

"When does the dance start?" Brooke asked as they walked into the Sweetery.

"Right now," Aly answered, standing at the back of the line.

Aly thought about what it would feel like to win an On the Ball trophy and how nervous some of the sixth graders must be now. But it was a good kind of nervous, she figured—the way you feel right before you open a present you've hoped for and dreamed about getting.

eleven

Good Knight

After Aly and Brooke ate their treats—a peanut butter cookie for Aly and a rainbow cookie covered with chocolate sprinkles for Brooke—the girls quickly walked back to True Colors.

"Mom, Mom, you'll never believe what we saw," Brooke blurted out. "It looks like Princess Polish might be closing!"

Mom looked at Joan, her eyebrows raised. "Well, that's interesting. Let's see if they open for business tomorrow," she said.

But that wasn't the only news. As Mom and Joan were cleaning up, they had discovered a canvas bag in the back room. "Aly, we found this in Sparkle Spa," Mom announced, holding it up. "Did one of your customers leave it? There are trophies inside."

Miss Gonzales! That bag was Miss Gonzales's! She had been holding it when she ran into Sparkle Spa after Maxie screamed. She was the teacher in charge of the Fall Ball and the awards. Aly gulped. "They're for the On the Ball winners!" she said.

"Oh no!" Brooke cried. "What if they can't announce the winners because there aren't any trophies? Because the trophies are *here,* in True Colors, instead of *there,* where they should be!"

"Where should they be?" Joan asked.

"At school!" Brooke and Aly said together.

"Well," Mom said, "it's almost time to go anyway. I'll drive you over to Auden."

"Go, go," Joan said, shooing all three of them out the door. "I'll lock up here."

On the way to school, Brooke could hardly sit still. "Hey, Aly," she said. "Do you know what this means?"

Aly shook her head.

"It means we get to go to the Fall Ball." Brooke's smile was so huge, it seemed to take up half her face.

Aly grinned. "You're right." Even though she was pretty sure her smile wasn't as big as Brooke's, Aly couldn't wait to see how everything looked.

"I'll wait right here," Mom told them as she pulled up to the curb. "In and out, so we can get home to Dad and Sparkly and dinner."

"In and out!" Brooke said. "We promise." She took Aly's hand, and they scooted out of the car. They ran toward the entrance, straight into Mr. Thomas, the security guard.

"Good evening, girls. Where are you going?" he asked. "I don't think either of you is old enough to be going to the dance."

Aly held out the bag with the trophies inside. "We're making a delivery."

"A very important one," Brooke added. "It's the trophies for the On the Ball winners. Miss Gonzales left them at our nail salon."

"I see," Mr. Thomas said. "That *is* very important. Let me lock the door and escort you in."

Aly, Brooke, and Mr. Thomas walked down the second-grade hallway, past the nurse's office, and into the gym. Aly and Brooke paused in the doorway.

The gym didn't look anything like a gym.

The balloons had covered all the lights, so the whole room had a purple and gold glow.

The glitter on the posters sparkled, and the streamers swayed gently back and forth.

There was also some sort of machine that blew bubbles from under the stage.

And Mr. Mehta, the music teacher, was up on the stage with big speakers and a computer.

"Wow," Brooke said breathlessly.

"Whoa," Aly said. It was even more beautiful than she'd imagined. Then she focused on all the sixth graders. They looked so fancy and grown-up. She spotted Anjuli in her bright purple dress. And Bethany and Mia. Then she saw Jenica in her Good Knight–colored dress dancing with Lee, one of the boys who had come into Sparkle Spa earlier that day.

"Okay, enough looking, we have to go deliver the trophies." Aly said to Brooke.

It felt funny to walk into the ball wearing shorts and a T-shirt, but Aly did it anyway. She looked around the edges of the gym for teachers and finally spotted

Miss Gonzales, then headed straight toward her. Miss Gonzales was talking to an adult Aly didn't know.

"Miss Gonzales, Miss Gonzales," Aly shouted over Mr. Mehta's loud music.

Miss Gonzales looked up.

Aly held out the bag. "I think you left these at True Colors today."

"I—oh!" Miss Gonzales said, taking the bag from Aly. "*That's* where I left them! Thank you so much for bringing them over. I've been going crazy trying to find my bag . . . and trying to figure out where I could find another set of trophies somewhere else in the school."

Aly smiled. "Happy to help."

She was about to turn and leave when Brooke said, "Um, Miss Gonzales, are you announcing the winners soon? Do you think maybe you could do it right *now*?"

Aly couldn't believe Brooke! But it would be nice if they could hear the announcements.

"Actually, it's almost time anyway," Miss Gonzales said. "And now that I have the trophies, I don't think anyone would mind if I sped things up by a few minutes."

She walked up on the stage and spoke to Mr. Mehta. The music got softer, and Miss Gonzales tapped the top of a microphone.

"Hi, sixth graders!" she said.

"Hi, Miss Gonzales!" a few of them answered.

Miss Gonzales held the microphone a little closer to her mouth. "As you all know, winning an On the Ball trophy at Auden is a very big honor. These trophies go to two members of our community—one boy and one girl—who embody the Auden spirit of helping others.

"So many of you sixth graders have worked on wonderful community projects this year, from fund-raising to tutoring to food drives and toy drives. I wish every single one of you could win a trophy.

"But there are two students whose projects stood out as exemplary to all the teachers. And they are: Jenica Posner, for promoting team building and sharing knowledge through Superstar Sports, and Oliver Shin, for focusing on those less fortunate and changing school policy through the Helping the Hungry at Lunch program!"

Along with the rest of the kids at the dance, Aly cheered for Jenica. She cheered for Oliver, too, even though, personally, she would have picked Cute Lucas for his Reading Buddies project.

Next to Aly, Brooke was jumping up and down, yelling, "Yay, Jenica! Three cheers for Jenica!"

Jenica and Oliver walked to the stage, and Miss Gonzales presented them with the trophies. Then Mr. Mehta started playing the school song on his keyboard, and all the kids—including Aly and Brooke—sang along.

The sixth graders grabbed hands and formed a circle that was almost as big as the whole gym. When they got to the last line of the Auden Elementary song—*"And we will always love our community"*—everyone raised their clasped hands in the air and shouted: "Go, Auden!" Then they clapped and cheered. It was one of the coolest things Aly had ever seen.

Even though Aly and Brooke weren't sixth graders, they both felt like they were part of the celebration. After all, a lot of those hands that had been raised in the air a moment ago had been in Sparkle Spa that afternoon. Knowing that they had contributed to the Fall Ball—just in this small way—made them feel proud and a part of something bigger than themselves—their community.

Aly had to admit, it was a pretty magical feeling.

How to Give Yourself (or a Friend!) a Caramel-Dipped Pedicure
By Aly (and Brooke!)

* . . * * . . * * . * * . * * . . *

What you need:

Paper towels

Polish remover

Cotton balls

Clear nail polish

Two colors of polish (I recommend purple and
    green; Brooke recommends pink and yellow)

What you do:

1. Put some paper towels on the floor so you don't
have to worry about spilling polish. (Actually, you
might want to do two layers. Once, I spilled
so much that it went through the first layer.
But I don't do that anymore.)

2. Take one cotton ball and put some polish remover on it. If you have polish on your toes already, use enough to get it off. If you don't, just rub the remover over your toenails to get off any dirt that might be on there. (Sometimes there's sock fuzz on your toenails. Gross, I know.)

3. Rip off two paper towels. Twist the first one into a long tube and weave it back and forth between your toes to separate them a little bit. Then do the same thing with the second paper towel on your other foot. You might need to tuck in the paper around your pinkie toe if it pops up and gets in your way while you polish.

4. Start with a coat of clear polish on each nail. (You can do your toes in any order you want. Aly and I like going from big toe to pinkie toe.)

Then don't forget to close up the polish bottle tightly when you're done.

5. Open up the polish color that you want to be the main one for all your nails. Paint it on. (You should be a little more careful with this color than with the clear, to make sure you don't get it on your skin.)

6. Fan your toes a little to dry them a bit, and then repeat step five, adding a second coat. (Remember, be careful! And close the polish when you're done.)

7. Once your toenails are dry, open the second color—the one you want your big toes to look "dipped" in—and wipe the brush on the side of the bottle opening so it's not drippy at all. Then,

very carefully, paint a straight line across the top of your right big toe, then the left. (Try not to let your hand wobble much so the line will be straight.)

8. Fan your big toes, drying them a bit before you apply a top coat of clear polish to all your toenails. Again, be sure to close the bottle up tight.

9. Now you have to let your toes fully dry. You can fan them with a magazine or use a nail dryer if you have one or sit and make a piece of jewelry or read a book or watch TV or talk to your friend. It usually takes about twenty minutes, but it could take longer. (After twenty minutes, check the polish by really lightly touching the stripe on your big toe with your fingertip. If it still feels sticky, let your toes dry longer so they don't get smudged!)

And now you have a beautiful caramel-dipped pedicure! Even after the polish is dry, it's a good idea not to wear socks or closed-toe shoes for a while. Bare feet or sandals are best so that all your hard work doesn't get smooshed. (Besides, that way, you can show people how fancy your toes look!)

Happy polishing!

✳ . ✴ . ✳ . ✳ . ✳ . ✴ . ✳

Goddess Girls

READ ABOUT ALL YOUR FAVORITE GODDESSES!

#1 ATHENA THE BRAIN | #2 PERSEPHONE THE PHONY | #3 APHRODITE THE BEAUTY | #4 ARTEMIS THE BRAVE

#5 ATHENA THE WISE | #6 APHRODITE THE DIVA | #7 ARTEMIS THE LOYAL | #8 MEDUSA THE MEAN | SUPER SPECIAL: THE GIRL GAMES

#9 PANDORA THE CURIOUS | #10 PHEME THE GOSSIP | #11 PERSEPHONE THE DARING | #12 CASSANDRA THE LUCKY

EBOOK EDITIONS ALSO AVAILABLE

From Aladdin
KIDS.SimonandSchuster.com

Candy Fairies

| Chocolate Dreams | Rainbow Swirl | Caramel Moon | Cool Mint | Magic Hearts |

| Gooey Goblins | The Sugar Ball | A Valentine's Surprise | Bubble Gum Rescue | Double Dip |

Jelly Bean Jumble   The Chocolate Rose   A Royal Wedding   Marshmallow Mystery

Visit candyfairies.co for more delicie fun with your favorite fairies

Play games, download activities, and so much more!